Courtney
the Clownfish
Fairy

To Emma Clerkin, a very
special friend of the fairies!

Special thanks
to Sue Mongredien

No part of this work may be reproduced, stored in a retrieval system, or transmitted in any form or by any means, electronic, mechanical, photocopying, recording, or otherwise, without written permission of the publisher. For information regarding permission, write to Rainbow Magic Limited c/o HIT Entertainment, 830 South Greenville Avenue, Allen, TX 75002-3320.

ISBN 978-0-545-27043-4

All rights reserved. Published by Scholastic Inc., 557 Broadway, New York, NY 10012, by arrangement with Rainbow Magic Limited.

SCHOLASTIC, LITTLE APPLE, and associated logos are trademarks and/or registered trademarks of Scholastic Inc. RAINBOW MAGIC is a trademark of Rainbow Magic Limited. Reg. U.S. Patent & Trademark Office and other countries. HIT and the HIT logo are trademarks of HIT Entertainment Limited.

12 11 10 9 8 7 6 5 4 3 2 1   11 12 13 14 15 16/0

Printed in the U.S.A.   40

This edition first printing, March 2011

Courtney
the Clownfish
Fairy

by Daisy Meadows

LITTLE
APPLE

SCHOLASTIC INC.

New York   Toronto   London   Auckland

Sydney   Mexico City   New Delhi   Hong Kong

The Fairyland Palace

GALA
FAIRYLAND ROYAL AQUARIUM

Fairyland Royal Aquarium

Kirsty's Gran's House

Lighthouse

The Park

Tide pool

Ocean Star Sailing Ship

Lea-On-Sea

Whales

Jack Frost's
Ice Castle

Ocean World
Sealife Center

Seals   Dolphins ↗

Baby
Turtles

Leamouth Pier

Penguins ↘   Ice floes

South Pole

With the magic conch shell at my side,
I'll rule the oceans far and wide!
But my foolish goblins have shattered the shell,
So now I cast my icy spell.

Seven shell fragments, be gone, I say,
To the human world to hide away,
Now the shell is gone, it's plain to see,
The oceans will never have harmony!

Contents

Where's Courtney?

"I can't believe that we're going home tomorrow," Rachel Walker said, gazing out to sea. "This has been such a terrific vacation!"

"I know," her best friend, Kirsty Tate, agreed. "I'll never forget it."

The two girls leaned against the railing at the end of Leamouth Pier. It was a warm, clear day and the sun cast dancing sparkles on the water below. Bouncy music boomed out from the carnival behind them.

Kirsty and Rachel had been staying with Kirsty's gran for a week of their spring vacation, and it had been a very exciting time. They had met the seven Ocean Fairies and enjoyed some wonderful adventures with them as they tried to

find the lost pieces of the magic golden conch shell.

Rachel sighed. "I'm a little worried. We still haven't found the last piece of the conch shell, and time's running out."

"We can't let our vacation end without finding it," Kirsty replied. "I really hope we meet Courtney the Clownfish Fairy soon!"

Kirsty and Rachel had met the Ocean Fairies on the first day of their trip. They'd been invited to the special Ocean Gala in Fairyland.

Every year at the party, Shannon the Ocean Fairy played a song on the magic golden conch shell. It ensured happy times in and around the oceans for everyone. But this year, before she could play the song, Jack Frost had crashed the party. He said he hated the ocean. He didn't like seeing anyone enjoy themselves, and he couldn't stand getting sand between his toes! He'd ordered his goblins to seize the golden conch shell. Unfortunately, they'd fought over it and then dropped it.

The shell had smashed into seven pieces. Before the Ocean Fairies could

grab them, Jack Frost used his magic
to send the shell pieces into the human
world. Luckily, the fairy queen had acted
quickly. She sent the Ocean Fairies'
seven magic creatures — a dolphin, a
seal, a penguin, a turtle, a starfish, a
whale, and a clownfish — out into the
human world, too. They would find and
protect each piece of the shell. So far,
Kirsty and Rachel had helped six of the
Ocean Fairies find their magic creatures
and the hidden pieces of the conch shell.
They still needed to find Courtney's
clownfish and the seventh piece of shell.

Until the shell was put back together,
the girls knew there would be chaos all
throughout the oceans.

The girls gazed at the carnival rides,
hoping they might see the little fairy.

There was a giant spiral slide, a bouncy castle, a spinning octopus ride, and lots of game booths. "Is that a sparkle of fairy dust near the slide?" Kirsty asked, pointing.

Rachel shaded her eyes to see. "No," she replied sadly. "It's just the flash from a camera." She linked her arm with Kirsty's. "It's no use for us to search for Courtney," she continued. "Remember what Queen Titania always says? We don't need to look for fairy magic. It will find its way to us."

Kirsty nodded. "You're right," she said. "Come on, let's go to the carnival. Look, there's a clown over there."

The girls wandered closer to the clown. He was wearing a red-and-white polka-dotted jumpsuit, a little black hat with a yellow flower on top, huge floppy shoes, and full clown makeup. He was busy bending balloons into shapes. The girls watched as he turned a red balloon into a dog for a little girl, and a blue balloon into a sword for a boy.

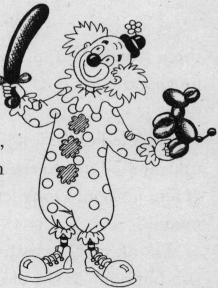

The clown saw

them watching and waved. "Hello!"
he called. "Let me make something for
you."

He pulled out a long orange balloon
and twisted it into the shape of a fish.
"Here you go! Don't let him swim
away!"

"Thank you," Kirsty said, taking the
fish balloon. As the clown walked away,

Kirsty's heart skipped excitedly.

A magical glimmer was coming from inside the balloon. As she looked closer, she realized it was Courtney the Clownfish Fairy!

Underwater Fun

Courtney waved from inside the balloon.
Then, with a little burst of sparkles,
she magically appeared in front of the
girls. She had long, wavy, red hair,
held back from her face with a pretty
purple headband. She wore a leaf-and–

fish patterned shirt over black leggings.
"Hello there," she said, as she hovered in
midair, her beautiful wings glittering in
the sunshine. "I'm glad I found you two.
I really need your help."

She landed lightly on Rachel's shoulder,
and Rachel smiled
as Courtney's
wings tickled
her neck. "Of
course we'll help,"
Rachel replied. "Let's
go somewhere where
it's not so crowded.
We don't want
anyone to see you."

Kirsty and Rachel walked to an area
of the pier that was less busy. An older

couple relaxed in beach chairs, arm-in-arm, but nobody else was around.

"That's better," Courtney said, her tiny fairy voice like tinkling bells. "We've got to find Squirt, my clownfish, and the last piece of the golden conch shell. The oceans are still a mess. As soon as we get the shell back together, Shannon can play her special song on it, and everything will go back to normal."

"What are we waiting for?" Kirsty said excitedly. "Let's start looking!"

Courtney grinned. "Just what I was hoping you'd say!" She giggled and

waved her wand at Kirsty and Rachel. Bright orange fairy dust surrounded them and the girls felt themselves shrinking down, down, down until they were fairies themselves!

Rachel fluttered her wings, loving how she felt lighter than air now. But the sea breeze sweeping in was strong. It was hard to hover in one place with it blowing her around!

"Now for some magic bubbles," Courtney said. She waved her wand

again. Two orange-tinted bubbles
appeared over Kirsty and Rachel's heads,
then vanished with
a *pop*! Kirsty
and Rachel
knew that
they would
be able to
breathe
underwater
now.

"Let's go to a special tropical part of
the ocean!" Courtney cried, waving her
wand a third time. A stream of sparkling
fairy dust poured from it and swirled all
around the three fairies.

Moments later, they were lifted up by
a glittering whirlwind that spun them

away from Leamouth Pier, so fast that
Rachel and Kirsty could barely see
a thing.

When the whirlwind came to a stop,
the girls found themselves in warm blue
water, right above the seabed. They were
surprised to discover an amazing sight.

"It's an underwater carnival!"
Kirsty said. "Look, there's an octopus
ride—with a real, live octopus!"

She giggled as she watched the octopus spin around very fast, with fish and other sea creatures perched on the ends of its arms.

"Look at the baby turtles," Rachel cried. A giant clam opened and closed nearby, blowing bubbles on which a group of baby turtles happily bounced. "They've got their very own version of a bouncy castle!"

The girls marveled at everything that was going on. There were sea creatures gathered together from all around the world—from coral reefs to polar seas, and all the oceans in between. Penguins and seals zoomed down a huge column of rock that looked just like a giant slide. Whales and dolphins flipped and spun, as if they were performing gymnastics. Other creatures seemed to be dancing in front of the flashing lights created by a group of lanternfish.

"Wow," Kirsty said, unable to take her eyes off the happy animals. "They're all having so much fun!"

"I could stand here all day watching them," Rachel said, mesmerized by the scene.

Courtney, however, didn't look so happy. *"Hmmm,"* she said. "I'm glad the sea creatures are enjoying themselves, but a lot of them shouldn't be in this part of the ocean! The penguins should be closer to the South Pole, the dolphins should be in cooler seas, and the whales normally need much deeper water than this." She frowned. "It's all because the last piece of shell is still missing. We've got to find it—and fast!"

Here Comes Trouble!

Luckily, the next moment, Courtney spotted something that put a smile on her face. "There's Squirt!" she cried, pointing at a nearby rock. The rock was covered with purple and red anemones. There was a whole group of clownfish playing a game of "catch-me-if-you-can" with them. The clownfish would dart into the anemones, and the anemones would try to close their fronds around them before the clownfish zipped out again.

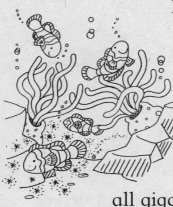

Rachel smiled as she watched them play. The clownfish were so pretty with their bright orange and white stripes. They all giggled as the anemones tried to catch them. One of the clownfish spotted Courtney and his face lit up in a huge grin. He swam over at once. It was Squirt!

Courtney beamed and threw her arms around him. "I've missed you, too," she said. "But it looks like you've made lots of friends here."

Squirt nodded. "He's also found the piece of conch shell," Courtney reported a minute later. "It's in one of the anemones. Come on!"

Squirt began swimming back toward the anemones. The three fairies were just about to follow when a chill spread through the ocean. The sea creatures stopped playing and looked around in surprise. The anemones and clams closed up tightly, as if they were scared.

"What's happening?" Kirsty

whispered, feeling goose bumps spring up on her arms and legs.

"I don't know," Courtney replied, shivering. "It's usually so warm here. I wonder if a stray iceberg floated this way because of the broken conch shell."

She stopped speaking as a long, thin shape appeared on the surface of the water above them, completely blocking out the last rays of sunlight.

Everyone stared up at it. For a second,

Rachel thought the shape was a massive whale, but then she realized it wasn't a living creature at all.

"It's a submarine!" Kirsty gasped.

The three fairies and the ocean creatures stared at the submarine in silence as it descended toward them.

The sub was an icy blue color. Icicles hung from its base and frost speckled the windows. On the side, in large jagged letters, was painted THE FROSTY DIVER.

Kirsty's stomach lurched as she read the words. *The Frosty Diver?* Did that mean the submarine had something to do with Jack Frost and his goblins?

"Oh, no," Courtney murmured, clearly thinking the same thing as Kirsty. "Here comes trouble."

The submarine continued to sink through the water. Finally, it came to

a halt and Kirsty and Rachel heard its
engine turn off.

"What's going to happen now?"
Rachel whispered nervously, her heart
thumping. "Should we hide?" She was
scared of Jack Frost. He could work
powerful icy magic and he was always in
a bad mood.

Courtney squeezed her hand. "Let's
wait and see what happens," she said
bravely.

The submarine's hatch flipped open, and the three fairies held their breath. The sea creatures were also silent. They all waited to see what would emerge from the submarine.

Out clambered a goblin, wearing huge floppy flippers and an icy breathing bubble over his head. He was followed by a second goblin, and then a third, and then a fourth . . . and even more goblins,

until there were at least ten of them standing by the submarine.

Kirsty let out a breath. Surely there couldn't be room for any more goblins in the submarine! Finally, one last figure climbed out. Even with his bubble helmet on, there was no mistaking the spiky ice crown on his head, or the wicked look on his face. It was Jack Frost!

A Race for the Shell

Jack Frost's cold, piercing eyes fell on the three nervous fairies and he gave a gloating laugh. "*Ahh*, so you're here," he sneered. "I should have known. Well, that doesn't bother me. My goblins and I are going to find the last piece of the conch shell before you do!"

"No, you won't," Courtney said.
"We'll find it first!"

Jack Frost laughed again, the scornful
sound ringing out through the water. "I
don't think so," he replied. "Goblins! To
work! Find that piece of shell, or you'll
all be in big trouble!"

The goblins leaped to obey and began
swimming in all directions, searching
for the shell. Some peered under leafy
seaweed plants, others dug through
the sand, and one silly goblin even
lifted a seal's flipper to peer
underneath it! The seal
glared at him before
swimming away with
its nose in the air.

Kirsty expected Courtney to make a dive for the anemones, but to her surprise, the fairy stayed still. "Shouldn't we go and get the shell?" Kirsty whispered.

Courtney shook her head and leaned over so that both girls could hear her reply. "Not right now," she said softly. "Jack Frost has his eye on us. If we swim straight for the anemones, he'll know that the shell piece is there. With so many goblins here, we'd be surrounded within seconds."

"We'll have to distract him somehow,"

Rachel said thoughtfully, watching as one of the goblins tickled a giant clam to make it open. The goblin peered inside the clam, looking for the piece of shell. He backed away quickly when the

clam shell almost slammed shut on his long nose!

Rachel turned back to the conversation. Now she was the one getting distracted! But maybe that was the answer.

"I just thought of something," she

whispered to Kirsty and Courtney. "What if we could get the carnival going again? Remember how we couldn't stop looking at it, Kirsty? Hopefully it would have the same effect on the goblins and Jack Frost. When they're distracted by all the carnival attractions, we can sneak over to the anemones and find the piece of golden conch shell!"

"That's a great idea," Courtney said. She motioned Squirt to swim over. She explained the plan to him in a low voice.

"Squirt, we need you to swim around and ask all the creatures to start up the carnival again. Tell them to make it look as exciting as possible!" She grinned. "I'll do my part to help with some fairy magic, too."

Squirt swam through the water like a bright orange streak of light to spread the word. Slowly, the carnival came back to life. The lanternfish began shining their lights, the octopus wiggled its arms, and the seals started racing down the giant slide again.

"Let's see what else we can do,"

Courtney said, waving her wand in
a complicated pattern. Orange fairy
dust swirled from it, and several new
attractions sprang up. There was a booth
with shells to knock down, a Tug-of-
War tent with a thick rope of seaweed to
pull, and a "Test Your Strength" tower.

"*Oooohhh!*" the goblins cried as they noticed what was happening.

"How cool is this?" one cheered, running to try the shell game.

"Fantastic!" another whooped, sprinting to a brand-new twisty slide. "Woo-hoo!" he squealed as he slid down it. "Come on, everyone, you have to try this!"

When all the goblins had abandoned the search for the shell, the fairies were able to swim over to the anemones where Squirt had said the conch piece was hidden. Squirt was still busily passing

on the message about the carnival plan,
so he wasn't there to show them exactly
which anemone the shell was hidden in.

"Let's look through them all," Kirsty
suggested, peering into the soft pink
fronds of the anemone closest to her. "It's
not in this one."

The fairies worked quickly, checking
through the anemones' fronds as fast as
they could. After only a few minutes,
they heard a triumphant shout from Jack
Frost.

"Aha! So that's where
the shell is—it's hidden
in the anemones!
Move over, fairies.
I'm going to find
that shell first. Just
watch me!"

Bouncing Bubbles

As Jack Frost strode along the seabed toward them, Rachel felt her spirits plunge. Oh, no! This was just what they were worried would happen!

Courtney wasn't about to give up
without a fight, though. She waved
her wand, sending a shower of sparkles
whirling toward Jack Frost. The
glittering sparkles circled some giant
clams near him, which blew out bubbles.
But these weren't ordinary bubbles—

they were enormous,
magical bubbles!
They were so
big that they
knocked Jack
Frost off his
feet and sent
him bouncing
away!

Jack Frost furiously tried to pop the
bubbles with his wand, but the magic

was too strong. *Boing! Boing! Boing!*
Rachel and Kirsty couldn't help giggling
as he bounced from bubble to bubble. He
started to look a little seasick
from all the
motion!

"That's amazing,
Courtney!"
Rachel laughed.
"Now to find that
piece of the conch
shell!"

With Jack Frost getting farther and
farther away, the water began to feel
warmer, and the anemones started
opening and closing again. Squirt swam
over, and Courtney hugged him. "Just
in time! Can you tell us which anemone

43

has the hidden piece of the conch shell?"
she asked.

Squirt pointed a fin at one anenome,
then another. He looked confused!

The fairies heard a series of muffled
pops. They turned to see a furious-
looking Jack Frost shaking his fist at
them in the distance. "He's managed to
burst the bubbles," Kirsty realized. "Now
he's heading this way—quick, guys!
We've got to find that shell right NOW!"

Just as Rachel was starting to lose hope, she suddenly noticed that the frond tips of one sea anemone were sparkling faintly. Could that be because the conch shell was hidden there?

She swam over to look, her heart thumping. When the anemone opened up again, she carefully dipped her hand inside. Her fingers closed around something hard and smooth. It was the seventh piece of the magic golden conch shell!

She pulled it out, feeling a huge wave

of relief. "I've got it!" she called to Kirsty and Courtney. "I found it!"

"Good job!" Courtney cried, her eyes bright with happiness. "Terrific, Rachel!"

Jack Frost shouted angrily when he saw the shining piece of shell in Rachel's hand. He was closing in on them. He glared and raised his wand.

An icy bolt of magic sped through the water from Jack Frost's wand and hit the piece of shell with a smack, immediately encasing it in ice.

"*Ow!*" Rachel cried, her hand stinging from the sudden cold. Before she knew what she was doing, she had dropped the piece of shell! An icy hand stretched forward to snatch it.

"I'll take that, thank you very much!" snapped Jack Frost.

But a brave little Squirt flapped a fin to beckon his friends, and a whole group of clownfish launched themselves at Jack Frost.

Jack Frost looked taken aback at this orange-and-white army that had appeared from out of nowhere. As the clownfish began to tickle him all over, he let out a surprised giggle.

Rachel and Kirsty stared in amazement as the clownfish flipped their ticklish fins and tails behind Jack Frost's knees, under his chin, and around his ears. Some even swam down to tickle his toes. The two friends had never seen Jack Frost laugh so hard! It was quite a sight to see him squirming helplessly from all the tickling.

"Ooh! Ha ha ha! Hoo-hoo-hoo! Stop!

Ha ha ha, stop!" He wailed, trying and failing to get away from the fish. Before long, he was completely weak from laughter. He tried to cling onto the piece of ice which contained the shell, but he finally lost his grip on it when the clownfish began tickling his stomach. The fairies saw the ice piece drop from his fingers, and all of them swooped to catch it. This was their chance!

All Together Now

Kirsty got to the chunk of ice first and managed to grab it. But it was still so freezing cold, she couldn't hold onto it.

Luckily, Courtney was able to use her magic to melt the ice around the fragment of shell. Quickly, she transformed it back to its Fairyland size.

"We did it!" Courtney cried happily. She hugged Rachel and Kirsty, holding onto the shell tightly. "Come on, Squirt, you can leave him alone now. We're going back to Fairyland!"

Squirt swam over to his fairy friend. She gave him a big kiss and then shrank him back down to his Fairyland size.

Jack Frost could only scowl, knowing he was beaten.

"Never mind, Your Frostiness," one of

the goblins said to him sympathetically. "Come and take a turn on the twisty slide. It's so much fun!"

Jack Frost made a sour face. "Fun? I thought I told you, nothing about the ocean is fun, in my opinion. Although. . . ." His eyes widened as he saw the octopus ride spinning around, its eight passengers all squealing with excitement. "I suppose that *could* be . . . enjoyable."

Jack Frost hurried off to join the goblins and Rachel was sure she saw an eager gleam in his eyes. She smiled to herself. Maybe Jack Frost was about to find out that the ocean was a fun place, after all!

But now it was time for Courtney and the girls to leave. Courtney waved her wand, taking all of them back to Fairyland in another sparkling whirlwind.

It wasn't long before the whirlwind cleared, setting them gently on the ground. Kirsty and Rachel saw that they were back in the majestic hall of the Fairyland Royal Aquarium. Squirt was back in his fish tank. King Oberon, Queen Titania, Shannon the Ocean Fairy, and the other six Ocean Fairies were all gathered around, as if they'd been waiting for Courtney, Kirsty, and Rachel's return.

When the crowd of fairies saw the golden piece of the conch shell in Courtney's hands, a huge cheer went up from everyone. The six ocean creatures all swam around excitedly in their tanks as they saw that their friend Squirt was also safely back in Fairyland.

Shannon rushed over, her eyes shining with happiness. "You found it!

Congratulations, all of you!" She took the shell piece gently from Courtney, then stepped over to where the other six pieces had been put together. She fitted the last piece carefully in place, and there was a flurry of golden sparkles. All seven fragments of the shell were magically joined back together, as if the shell had never even been broken!

With a big smile, Shannon raised the conch shell to her lips and played a beautiful melody that sent shivers down Rachel and Kirsty's spines.

The hall was quiet as everyone listened. Once Shannon had finished, however, another cheer erupted, and all the fairies burst into applause.

"So everything in the oceans will go back to the way it should be," Shannon said, beaming proudly. "Thanks to the Ocean Fairies, and our very special helpers!"

Kirsty and Rachel blushed with pride. "We enjoyed every minute of it," Kirsty said.

"I'm glad to hear it," the queen said. "We'd like to thank you for all your help with a little gift."

"We hope they'll remind you of your ocean adventures," King Oberon said. He smiled as he gave each of the girls a present, wrapped in gold paper and tied with a blue ribbon.

Kirsty and Rachel unwrapped the presents to find that they'd each been given a smaller version of the magic golden conch shell. "It's beautiful, thank you!" Rachel cried, gazing at the shiny, sparkling shell in her hands.

Queen Titania smiled. "Whenever you raise the shell to your ear, you'll be able to hear Shannon's special song," she said. "That way, you'll never forget how you helped us save the oceans."

"Thank you. We love helping our fairy friends," Kirsty said, holding the shell to her ear and listening to its beautiful music. "Well, we love being friends with you," Queen Titania replied, "although I'm sad to say it's time for you to return to your own world now. We hope we'll see you again very soon!"

The girls hugged all their fairy friends

good-bye. Then Queen Titania threw
a handful of sparkling fairy dust over
them. The glittering whirlwind appeared
one last time. It dropped them right back
where they'd been standing on Leamouth
Pier when the adventure began. They
were regular girls again, without their
beautiful fairy wings, but they still had
their pretty shell gifts.

"There you are!" said a voice. Rachel and Kirsty turned to see Kirsty's gran bustling along the pier toward them. "I can't believe our week together is almost over. I hope you haven't been too bored staying here with me."

"Bored? Not at all!" Kirsty said. "We've had a fantastic time."

"I've loved staying with you by the beach," Rachel added.

Splash! As the three of them gazed out to sea, a pod of dolphins suddenly leaped from the water, surprising them all.

"Now there's a treat for your last day here," Kirsty's gran said happily. "It's not every day that you see dolphins, is it?"

Kirsty and Rachel shared a secret smile as they watched the playful dolphins. This week, they'd seen whales, penguins, octopuses, seals—all kinds of amazing sea creatures! But it probably wasn't a good idea to tell Kirsty's gran that. "The ocean is a magical place," Kirsty replied instead, gazing out at the water happily. "A truly magical place!"

RAINBOW magic™

THE NIGHT FAIRIES

The Ocean Fairies have found all the
pieces of the magic golden conch shell—
now Rachel and Kirsty must help
the Night Fairies!

Join their next magical adventure
in this special sneak peek of

Ava

the Sunset Fairy!

Strange Sunset

"Look, Kirsty!" Rachel Walker said
excitedly to her best friend, Kirsty Tate.
It was a warm summer evening, and the
girls were standing on the deck of a little
red-and-white ferry as it chugged along
the winding river. "I don't think we're far
from Camp Stargaze now."

Kirsty looked where Rachel was

pointing and saw a wooden sign on the river bank. The sign was in the shape of an arrow pointing downriver, and it said: THIS WAY TO CAMP STARGAZE.

"Hooray!" Kirsty beamed at Rachel. "I'm *really* looking forward to this vacation."

The girls and their parents were spending a week of summer break at Camp Stargaze together. Kirsty and Rachel were thrilled. Even though they were best friends, they didn't live near each other. So they loved meeting up during school vacation whenever they could.

"Not far to go now, girls," called Mr. Walker, Rachel's dad. He was leaning on the side of the boat with Mrs. Walker and Mr. and Mrs. Tate, watching the beautiful countryside pass by. The river was surrounded by open fields and rolling hills, with green trees here and there.

"Oh, look, girls!" Mrs. Tate exclaimed, gazing up at the sky. "The sun is setting. Isn't it pretty?"

All the passengers on deck, including Rachel and Kirsty, looked up, too. The sun was just beginning to sink slowly, streaking the blue sky with long ribbons of gold, orange, and pink. The light reflected down onto the river and the fields, bathing everything in a soft glow. The water looked like liquid gold!

"It's magical!" Rachel breathed, her eyes wide. Then she glanced at Kirsty and flashed her a secret smile.

Kirsty grinned back, knowing exactly what Rachel was thinking. She and

Rachel knew more about magic than anyone else in the whole world. They were friends with the fairies!

The girls had visited Fairyland many times, and had helped out their magical friends whenever they were in trouble. The fairies' biggest enemy was mean, grumpy Jack Frost. He was always trying to cause trouble in Fairyland and the human world. Rachel and Kirsty were never quite sure what trouble Jack Frost and his goblins would cause next!

Suddenly, Kirsty blinked. For a moment she'd thought the gold, orange, and pink colors of the setting sun were fading and changing into something different.

I must be imagining it, Kirsty thought. But then she looked again and was horrified to see that she was right! The beautiful colors *were* changing before Kirsty's eyes.

"What's happening?" Rachel asked. She'd noticed exactly the same thing, and so had everyone else on the ferry. They were all staring up at the sky in surprise.

"Look at the sunset," Kirsty cried. "It's turning *green*!"

A few seconds later, all the gold, pink, and orange had vanished completely. Now the sunset was casting a strange, spooky green glow on the landscape around it.

"Everything's green!" Kirsty went on in a shocked voice. "The sun, the fields, the ferry—everything!"

"And so are *we*!" Rachel pointed out, staring at Kirsty. All of the passengers, including the girls and their parents, were bathed in the same emerald-colored glow.

"We look like Jack Frost's goblins!" Kirsty whispered.

The girls' parents and the other grown-ups on the ferry were discussing what could have caused the strange sunset.

"Maybe it's just a trick of the light shining through the clouds," Mr. Tate suggested.

"Or maybe the sunset is reflecting off the river and the fields, and picking up that green color," said Mrs. Walker.

Rachel glanced at Kirsty. "I think there's something very strange going on here, Kirsty," she murmured.

"So do I," Kirsty agreed. "I wonder if it could be something *magical*?"

RAINBOW magic™

There's Magic in Every Series!

The Rainbow Fairies
The Weather Fairies
The Jewel Fairies
The Pet Fairies
The Fun Day Fairies
The Petal Fairies
The Dance Fairies
The Music Fairies
The Sports Fairies
The Party Fairies

Read them all!

■SCHOLASTIC

www.scholastic.com
www.rainbowmagiconline.com

HiT entertainment

RMFAIRY2

RAINBOW magic

These activities are magical!
Play dress-up, send friendship notes, and much more!

SCHOLASTIC
www.scholastic.com
www.rainbowmagiconline.com

RMACTIV3